ER1B

D0859354

GLEAM and GLOW

Written by
EVE BUNTING

Illustrated by
PETER SYLVADA

HARCOURT, INC.

Orlando   Austin   New York   San Diego   Toronto   London

Weld Library District
Greeley, CO 80634-6632

Special thanks to James B. Stewart, assistant headmaster at The Gillispie School in La Jolla, California, and to Allyn Johnston—E. B.

Text copyright © 2001 by Eve Bunting
Illustrations copyright © 2001 by Peter Sylvada

All rights reserved. No part of this publication may be reproduced or transmitted in any form or by any means, electronic or mechanical, including photocopy, recording, or any information storage and retrieval system, without permission in writing from the publisher.

Requests for permission to make copies of any part of the work should be submitted online at www.harcourt.com/contact or mailed to the following address: Permissions Department, Harcourt, Inc., 6277 Sea Harbor Drive, Orlando, Florida 32887-6777.

Photo credit: Michele Clement (illustration on page 5)

www.HarcourtBooks.com

Library of Congress Cataloging-in-Publication Data
Bunting, Eve, 1928–
Gleam and Glow/written by Eve Bunting; illustrated by Peter Sylvada.
p. cm.
Summary: After his home is destroyed by war, eight-year-old Viktor finds hope in the survival of two very special fish.
[1. War—Fiction. 2. Fishes—Fiction.] I. Sylvada, Peter, ill. II. Title.
PZ7.B91527Gl 2001
[E]—dc21   00-10005
ISBN 978-0-15-202596-0

P O N M L K J I H G

Printed in Singapore

The illustrations in this book were done in oils.
The display type was hand-lettered by Georgia Deaver.
The text type was set in Quadraat.
Color separations by Bright Arts Ltd., China
Printed and bound by Tien Wah Press, Singapore
Production supervision by Sandra Grebenar and Pascha Gerlinger
Designed by Judythe Sieck

For Dr. Andrea Karlin—E. B.

For Poncho—P. S.

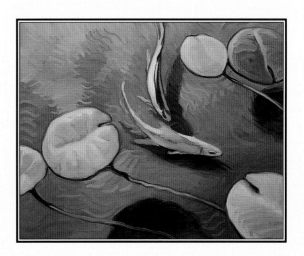

When Papa left to join the underground, Marina cried. To be truthful, Mama and I cried, too.

"I don't want Papa to be underground," Marina sobbed.

"Shh, little one," Mama said. "It just means he's fighting secretly with many of our men. On top of the ground."

I gave Marina a pitying glance. She's only five and doesn't know much. I'm eight, and I know a lot.

Before he left, Papa had tried to explain things to Marina.

"Why don't those people like us?" she'd asked.

I didn't know why, either, but I rolled my eyes and pretended I did.

"We're different from them," Papa told her. "They think this is their country and they don't want us living here. But this is *our* country. I will fight with the Liberation Army to stop them from pushing us out of our own land." He put his hand on my shoulder. "Viktor, you are the man of the house now. Be a strong help to your mother."

And then he was gone.

"I'll be back," he'd said. But I worried. What if he came back, and we weren't here?

Mama said we would have to leave soon. It was getting too dangerous to stay much longer. Our enemies were coming, sweeping through villages like great brooms, forcing people out and burning their homes.

Every day we heard distant gunshots and saw smoke rise into the faraway skies.

Every day strangers stopped on their way out of the country to put down their bundles, to share our food, to take shelter under our roof. They told terrible stories of how it had been for them and their neighbors when the soldiers came. They cried as they talked. Their eyes went this way and that, as if they thought the soldiers were just outside on our doorstep.

When their stories got too terrible, Mama sent Marina and me to the pond for fresh water or to the vegetable patch to look for hidden potatoes.

But we heard a lot anyway.

Marina started to suck her thumb again, and I wet the bed three nights in a row.

Mama held me close. "It's all right, Viktor. There is no harm done."

One day a family came on a tractor. They had a boy my age named Alexsa and a dog who could do tricks. Alexsa liked showing him off.

"My father is in the underground," I told him, and I felt proud. Having a father in the underground was better than having a dog who could do tricks.

I watched them leave the next morning. We don't have a tractor. I knew that when we left, we would have to walk.

A few days later a man came. His heavy bag was strapped on his back, and he was carrying a bowl with water and two fish in it. He put the bowl on our table, and it seemed to me that all the light of the world was trapped inside that glass bowl.

"I can't carry them farther," he said. "Will you keep them? They are very wondrous fish."

Mama shook her head. "We are leaving ourselves in a day or two."

Marina jumped up and down. "Please, Mama! Aren't they pretty? I've just thought up their names. Gleam and Glow."

The man sighed. "Let them stay behind when you go, then. An extra day or two of life is as important to a fish as it is to us. Here is their food." He gave Marina a twist of paper. "Sprinkle a little on top of the water each day."

"I will," Marina promised.

For two days she fed them and talked to them and even tried to pet them with her finger.

"I love Gleam and Glow," she told Mama. "I love them with all my heart."

Three days later Mama said we could wait no longer. "I wanted to stay till it got warmer," she said softly, as if to herself. "The cold will be hard on the little one." I knew she was remembering the pneumonia Marina had last year.

"We will leave tomorrow early," she said to us. "We must make it to the border and the safe country beyond."

"Is it far to walk?" I asked, wishing for a tractor.

"It is. But we will get there."

"Please, please, can we take Gleam and Glow?" Marina begged. "I'll carry them."

"You couldn't, Marina," Mama said. "We will have to leave them. But think, we may be able to find your father. Won't that be good?"

I thought maybe she was just trying to give us hope, but even the goodness of that hope didn't comfort Marina. She slept with Mama that night, and I heard her sobbing for a long time before it was quiet and I knew she was asleep.

I lay looking around my room, putting it in my memory. My books on the shelves Papa made for me. The painting I had done that Mama had framed. I thought about how hard it would be for Marina to leave her fish.

When the clock struck midnight I got up, carried the fishbowl outside to our pond, and slipped Gleam and Glow into the water. They flashed into the tangled weeds at the edge of the pond. I sprinkled what was left of their food on the water. "One or two extra days of life," I whispered. "Good luck."

We would need good luck, too.

Mama woke us at dawn. When I told about the fish, we went out to see if they made it through the night. Marina clapped her hands and called their names, but Gleam and Glow stayed out of sight.

"Maybe they're sleeping," she said. "I know they'll love our pond."

Our bundles were ready to carry. Two each for Mama and me and a smaller one for Marina.

The road outside our house was filled with half-light shadows. I looked back once as we walked away. There was our oak tree, the vegetable patch, Mama's flower garden, where the flowers waited under the earth for spring.

Would we ever come home again? Would Papa ever find us?

We walked and walked.

We were slow and people passed us. But some went at our pace, and the things they told us made us know that we had been right to leave before the horror reached out to us.

We walked and walked.

A man with a wheelbarrow let Marina ride on top for a whole day. He took one of Mama's bundles and one of mine. That was the best walking day ever.

At night we slept in fields or barns. One night it rained hard, but we were lucky to find a deserted house and we slept well.

Once some men from our Liberation Army stopped and shared chickens with us. We had chicken stew that night.

"Do you know our papa?" Marina asked. But they said they didn't.

We kept looking for Papa, thinking sometimes we saw him. But it was always a stranger who just looked like him.

Some days Marina and I begged to stop. We could go no farther. But Mama's will pulled us on.

And then, one morning, we heard cheers from people walking ahead of us. Someone shouted, "I see the border! We're almost there." All along the line everyone cheered until our throats hurt.

It was better after we crossed the border. There was a camp with tents for us to live in; there was food, and fires to cook it. We could wash our clothes and ourselves. There were other children in the camp. I made friends with two boys named Behar and Admir, and we played games together. We were allowed to paint the initials of the Liberation Army on a wall and we felt good, as if we were fighting alongside the liberators to set our country free.

We were in the camp for a long time, and that is where Papa found us. I looked up one evening and there he was, dirty and thin—but beautiful. Marina and I screamed with joy, and he picked us both up and kissed our faces over and over. Mama stood with tears running down her cheeks, and he gathered her close and whispered into her hair. She touched his face with her fingertips as if she thought he was just a dream. "Are you really here?"

"I am here," Papa said softly. "It's a miracle I found you. I asked and asked. Always I asked."

Marina tugged at his leg. "Can you stay, Papa?"

"Yes, little one." Papa smiled. I didn't know how he could stay. It was enough that he could.

"Can we go home now, Papa?" I asked.

"Not yet, Viktor. Soon."

But it was many months before we were told it was safe to leave. That night we all danced between the rows of tents. It was a great, joyful party.

The next day we started on the long walk home.

And, oh, it was sad. We saw no houses, no farms, no animals along the way, just rubble and great holes where bombs had fallen.

We walked and walked.

I knew our house would be gone. I didn't want to know that, but somehow I just did. Papa carried Marina on his shoulders and she jabbered happily. She was the only one who thought our old life would be waiting for us.

When I saw the oak tree still standing, my heart raced with hope. I clutched Mama's hand. Maybe it was going to be all right.

Then I looked beyond the tree. Our house was only a skeleton. A few flowers poked up from Mama's garden. Except for that, we could have been on the moon.

Marina was the first to remember the fish. She took a stale slice of bread from Mama's bundle and ran toward the pond, calling out Gleam and Glow's names. We ran behind to comfort her.

And there was our pond, as shimmery and dazzling as melted gold. It was filled with countless fish.

Mama pressed her hands to her heart. "Gleam and Glow and their children and their children's children," she said.

"They found their own nourishment," Papa said.

Marina clapped her hands. "Oh, what smart fish," she said.

"In spite of everything, they lived," Mama whispered.

Like us, I thought. *They lived*.

"Gleam! Glow!" Marina called, and tossed in crumbs of bread. Fish after fish came to the edge of the pond where she knelt. "Look!" She pointed. "There's Gleam and there's Glow."

That made us laugh, because those fish were as identical as could be.

"Did you miss me?" Marina asked them. "I missed you."

I leaned close to the water. "We're back, Gleam and Glow," I told the fish. "We've come home."

A NOTE FROM THE AUTHOR

There is a village called Jezero in Bosnia-Herzegovina. In 1990, before the Bosnian war, a villager named Smajo Malkoc gave his sons two golden fish in an aquarium.

When the war came, Malkoc's family fled from the Bosnian-Serb forces. In an attempt to save the fish, his wife released them into a nearby lake.

In 1995, when the family returned home after the war, they found their house and village in ruins. The lake, however, was teeming with life—it was filled with shining golden fish. Left alone, the fish had fed on the underwater lake life, thrived, and multiplied.

Hearing of the remarkable fish, people came to admire and to buy. The fish turned out to be not only beautiful but valuable. Prosperity and fame came to the Malkocs and their neighbors, and the village was rebuilt.

Gleam and Glow was inspired by this true and magical story. Yet my version is not only a story for a particular country or people—it's for people everywhere who have been forced from the lives they have known, and who find hope in the most unexpected places.